The Rescue Princesses

The Snow Jewel

More amazing
animal adventures!

The Secret Promise

The Wishing Pearl

The Moonlight Mystery

The Stolen Crystals

The Rescue Princesses

The Snow Jewel

💜 **PAULA HARRISON** 💜

Scholastic Inc.

For Billy, Freddie, and Martha

ISBN 978-0-545-50917-6

12 11 10 9 8 7 6 5 4 3 2 1   13 14 15 16 17 18/0

Printed in the U.S.A.   40
First printing, October 2013

CHAPTER ONE

Sledding at the Castle

Princess Freya sped across the crisp snow in her thick furry boots. Her blond braids bounced on her shoulders and her blue eyes shone brightly.

She ran through the gate at the end of the castle garden and closed it behind her. Then she stopped for a moment to gaze down the hill at the newly made ice rink at the bottom. Fresh snow had fallen in the night and the sunshine was making everything sparkle.

A group of princes raced out of the
gray stone castle behind her and began
throwing snowballs at one another. Freya
swung around to watch them. It was
strange seeing her castle so busy and
noisy when it was usually so quiet.

Her dad, King Eric, had invited all the
royal families from around the world to
come and spend the winter holidays here
in the kingdom of Northernland. The
ice rink had been dug out and smoothed
over especially for everyone to skate on.
The guests had arrived yesterday, and
now the castle was crammed with kings,
queens, princes, and princesses.

Freya took a few steps down the hill,
thinking about the other princesses.
She had been longing to meet some
girls her own age for what seemed like
forever. She'd seen four princesses slip
out the door after breakfast. They had

run off laughing together and she had desperately wanted to join them. But where had they gone?

The sound of giggling floated over to her on the frosty air. Freya hurried down the slope and through a cluster of fir trees, trying to see where the noise was coming from. When she reached the other side of the trees, she saw the girls right away.

Four princesses, wearing thick coats, woolen scarves, and gloves, were pulling a wooden sled up the hill. When they reached the top, a girl with wavy black hair sat down on the sled and the others gave her a huge push.

The princess on the sled zoomed away with a shout of delight. Halfway down the hill, she jumped on top of the sled and glided the rest of the way standing on one leg. Freya's eyes widened. She'd

never seen somebody do such a daring trick before!

The black-haired princess jumped off at the bottom of the slope, and the others ran down to help her pull the sled back up. A princess with red curls noticed Freya and waved.

"Hello!" called the red-haired princess. "Would you like to come and try?"

Freya blushed and ran over. "Thanks! That's really nice of you!"

"It's not really *that* nice!" The princess laughed. "We borrowed this sled from the castle. So it's really yours! I'm Princess Emily, by the way."

"And I'm Lulu," said the black-haired princess. "This is Jaminta." She pointed at a girl with smooth dark hair. "And that's Clarabel." She pointed at a girl with golden hair.

"Hello," said Jaminta and Clarabel, smiling widely.

"I'm Freya," said Freya shyly. "I'm so pleased that you've all come to stay. I've wanted to meet some other princesses for a long time."

"Didn't you come to the Mistberg Grand Ball last year?" asked Lulu, looking at Freya curiously.

Freya shook her head. "My dad likes to stay here at home in Northernland."

"Well, I think it's wonderful here in the snow." Emily smiled at her. "Would you like the next turn on the sled?"

Freya beamed back. "Yes, please!"

The five princesses grabbed the rope and pulled the sled up to the top of the hill. Then Freya got the sled into position and climbed on.

"Try going down backward," cried Lulu, jumping up and down. "It's really fun!"

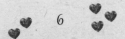

"All right! Here I go!" said Freya, turning around on the sled so that she was facing the wrong way.

"Are you ready?" asked Jaminta.

Freya glanced over her shoulder at the steep slope below. "Ready!" she said firmly.

Jaminta and Emily gave the sled a push to start her off. Freya raced down the slope at high speed, her blond braids flying behind her in the wind.

"Woo-hoo!" she shouted as she went faster and faster.

Suddenly, one corner of the sled tilted down, making the whole thing wobble. Freya slid forward. She grabbed ahold of the sides, desperately trying to keep her balance. But the sled tipped over, sending her flying.

She landed with a gasp in the middle of a deep snowdrift. The sled landed next

to her as she lay still, feeling the snow seeping down her neck.

"Oh, no! Are you OK?" Clarabel ran toward her.

Freya sat up and rubbed the snow away from her mouth. She felt a little dizzy, but not really hurt. "Yes, I'm all right," she said. "It was pretty funny, actually. For a second I felt like I was flying!"

Lulu pulled the sled upright and looked underneath. Then she scooped some snow out of a hollow. "There's a hole here. It's probably a rabbit's burrow. The sled runner must have gotten caught in it, and that's why the sled tipped over."

"The poor rabbits!" Freya got up and peered into the hollow. "I hope I didn't frighten them by sledding into their hole like that!"

Emily laughed. "I'm sure you didn't."

Lulu looked at Freya, who was covered in snow from head to foot. "I bet the rabbits are safe, deep down in their burrow. You look like you need the Rescue Princesses' help more than they do!" Then she stopped suddenly and clapped her hand over her mouth.

Emily and Clarabel glanced at each other, as if they didn't know what to do.

"Lulu! You weren't supposed to say that!" exclaimed Jaminta.

"Oops! I forgot!" Lulu's eyes grew wider.

"What's the matter?" asked Freya, seeing their startled looks. "Who *are* the Rescue Princesses?"

CHAPTER TWO

The Snow-Quartz Necklace

Emily pushed her red curls behind her ear and nudged Lulu. "I think we should tell her. It would be nice to have another princess to help us."

Lulu frowned. "But she *has* to love animals."

"And she has to keep it all a secret," added Jaminta.

"I'm good at keeping secrets," said Freya, shaking the snow off her braids.

"Do you really think we should tell?" said Jaminta doubtfully. "The Rescue Princesses might not work very well with five people."

"We could make it work if we all help each other," said Clarabel, and Emily nodded in agreement.

Freya watched them, a bubbly feeling rising inside her. *The Rescue Princesses!* It sounded so exciting! But what was it all about?

Lulu gave Freya a solemn look. "The four of us are the Rescue Princesses, and we'll tell you all about it if you're *sure* you really like animals."

"I do! I love them!" said Freya, her eyes lighting up.

"Can you prove it?" said Jaminta. "I mean, have you ever taken care of any animals?"

"Yes!" Freya beamed. "I've got some living in my bedroom right now! Come on, I'll show you."

The princesses followed Freya back toward the castle. The snow crunched beneath their boots and the sled skimmed along behind them. When they reached the castle door, they shook the snow off their coats and went inside.

In the Great Hall, the kings and queens were sitting in front of a crackling fire, sipping cups of coffee. There were golden streamers hanging from the ceiling and fairy lights twinkling at the windows. Freya had helped her dad with the decorations. She loved to see the castle looking so beautiful.

"My room's up here," she said, leading the princesses up the wooden staircase.

"What kind of animals do you have?" asked Emily.

Freya opened her bedroom door. "Come and see!"

"Where are they?" asked Lulu, gazing eagerly around the room. "Oh, look!"

The girls rushed over to a small box padded with woolly sweaters. Inside the box was a mother cat lying down with six sleepy kittens. They had their eyes shut tight as they snuggled together for warmth. Five of the kittens had beautiful black fur, the same as their mother's. The sixth kitten had white patches on its face and tummy, and four white paws. It opened its bright blue eyes and stared at the princesses.

"I made the box really comfy for them," said Freya happily. "I think they like it."

"They're lovely." Clarabel stroked the head of one little kitten. "Look at their tiny ears!"

Freya picked up the kitten with four

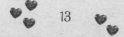

white paws and kissed her. "I call this one Minky. She's the naughty one. She's always bouncing around the room and hiding under the bed."

Minky gave a tiny meow and looked at the girls, as if she knew they were talking about her.

"Hello, Minky," said Jaminta, gently shaking one soft white paw.

Minky meowed back and swished her little tail.

"What are all the others named?" asked Lulu.

"The mother cat's Carla, and these are Dusky, Fluffles, Velvet, Coco, and Daisy," said Freya, pointing to the kittens one by one.

"Aw! Aren't they beautiful!" cried Emily.

The girls huddled around the box to stroke the kittens, who woke up and filled the room with their little meows.

"Tell me about the Rescue Princesses. I want to know everything." Freya sat down on the bed and hugged her kitten tightly. Minky flicked out a little pink tongue and licked her cheek.

"We met at the Mistberg Grand Ball, and there were some deer in trouble in the forest nearby," began Emily.

"So we rescued them all and we made a secret promise that we would always help any animal in trouble, even if it was dangerous," continued Lulu.

"And since then we've found lots more animals that have needed rescuing," said Jaminta. "And we use special rings to call each other if we're apart." She showed Freya her emerald ring and pressed it to make it glow.

"Wow!" breathed Freya. "And you do it all without any grown-ups helping?"

Emily nodded. "We train ourselves in things like climbing and balancing so that we can get better at the rescues."

"I can't believe you've done all of that. I'm hardly ever allowed to do things on my own," said Freya wistfully. "It all sounds amazing."

"So what should we do?" said Lulu, turning to the others. "Do we want Freya to join us?"

Freya watched them longingly. These weren't just girls the same age as her; they were girls who had adventures. She just *had* to join them!

"What is it that *you* want, Freya?" asked Clarabel.

"I would love to become a Rescue Princess, too . . . if that's all right?" Freya clasped her hands together hopefully. If only they would let her!

The others exchanged looks and smiled.

Lulu nodded. "If you really, really want to, then you *should* become a Rescue Princess. I bet we're going to have some awesome adventures together!"

"We haven't even told you about the ninja moves yet," said Emily, grinning.

"Ninja moves?" squeaked Freya.

Her squeal woke up Minky, who had been quietly snoozing. The little cat wriggled and got her paw caught in a pale blue ribbon that hung around Freya's neck. Finding her paw stuck, she wriggled even more.

"Hold still, Minky! You're making it worse." Freya untangled the kitten's paw and then put Minky down on the floor for a moment so that she could unknot the twisted ribbon.

"That's a lovely jewel." Jaminta stepped

closer to look at the beautiful white stone hanging on the end of Freya's ribbon.

Freya held up the roughly shaped gem. It dangled there, sparkling like a drop of snow. "This is a snow-quartz jewel. My mom left it to me. She died when I was a baby. My dad says she used to wear it all the time. I don't really remember because I was so little, but I'm glad she wanted it to be mine because it's so pretty."

"It's beautiful." Clarabel smiled.

"Thanks!" Freya tucked the blue ribbon away again. "My mom left me a note about it as well. It says my jewel is special and can protect me against ice and snow —"

"Hang on!" Emily interrupted. "Can anyone see Minky? I'm sure she was here a minute ago."

"Oh, not again! She scampered away yesterday, too. It took me forever to find her." Freya looked at the door and noticed it was half open. "We really should have closed that door. Quick, everyone! We must find her before she wanders off. If she gets lost among all the kings and queens she'll be so scared."

CHAPTER THREE

The King's Royal Slipper

Lulu dived under the bed, while Clarabel and Emily peered inside the dressers. Jaminta ran to the half-open door and looked down the hallway.

"Minky? Where are you?" called Freya.

Suddenly, there was a scrabbling noise and a large lump popped up underneath Freya's quilt. The lump started zigzagging across the bed in all directions.

"Minky! What are you doing?" Freya giggled. "How did you get under there?"

She lifted up the quilt and a little whiskery face poked out. Minky stuck out one white paw and then dived farther under the covers again.

"She's definitely an adventure cat!" said Lulu, grinning.

Freya scooped up Minky, who meowed in protest.

"Well, you can't stay under there!" said Freya, kissing the top of Minky's head.

Jaminta came back inside and closed the door. "Does she get into a lot of trouble?"

Freya nodded. "Now that she's growing bigger she likes to climb things and —" She broke off suddenly and listened.

A deep voice rumbled down the hallway, followed by footsteps and a knock on the door.

"Freya, are you there?" asked a man's voice.

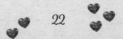

"That's my dad," said Freya, looking startled. She hurriedly put Minky back in the box with the other kittens, ran to the door, and opened it.

King Eric stood in the doorway. He had fair hair that was turning gray at the sides, and he wore a blue robe. On one foot he wore a brown slipper, but on the other he wore nothing but a stripy sock.

"Good morning, princesses," he said, with a small bow.

The princesses curtsied. "Good morning!"

The king turned to his daughter. "Freya, my dear, something awful has happened. Can you tell me anything about this terrible disaster?" He held up a large brown slipper, which obviously matched the one he was wearing.

"What's wrong with it, Dad?" asked Freya.

King Eric turned the slipper over to show her the bottom, which had a big round hole in it. "*This* is what's wrong! Something has destroyed my slipper completely. It's been nibbled until it's beyond repair and I bet one of these animals did it." He walked over to the box of kittens and peered at them disapprovingly. Then he noticed the sweaters inside the box. "Freya! Are you using your sweaters as a pillow for these cats?"

"They're only old sweaters," said Freya hurriedly. "And maybe it wasn't the kittens that nibbled your slipper. Maybe it was a mouse."

"A mouse!" exclaimed King Eric. "We do not have mice wandering around this castle. No, I'm sure it must have been one of these creatures."

"They seem like very sweet kittens, Your Majesty," said Emily.

Lulu and Clarabel nodded in agreement.

"My dear princesses, I understand why you like them," said the king, smiling at the girls, "but I cannot have animals making a mess everywhere."

Minky wiggled excitedly and bounced right out of the box. She skipped across the carpet to the king's feet and pounced on the slipper he was wearing as if it were a giant brown mouse. Meowing gleefully, she dug her little claws into the slipper and held on tight.

"You see! This is probably the very animal that made the hole," said the king, shaking his foot to try and dislodge the kitten. "Off you get now — silly cat!"

Minky gave the big brown foot mouse a friendly little nip before leaping away. Then she ran around and around the king's legs in a circle until he looked very dizzy.

"Stop it, Minky!" said Freya.

"Kittens should *not* be kept in bedrooms," said King Eric sternly. "In fact, they shouldn't be kept anywhere in the castle. What if they start chewing our guests' clothes and shoes? They *have* to be moved."

"Oh, no, Dad!" cried Freya, grabbing the scampering Minky. "Please don't move them. I'll make sure they don't ever leave my bedroom. Then they can't ruin anyone's clothes."

"No, Freya. I am not happy with them living here. They will be moved to the shed. They will be all right in there. I'll ask one of the servants to take them and to make sure that they're left with plenty of food and water." The king walked away, but stopped and turned around when he reached the door.

"I saw you sledding from the window, Freya," he added. "I don't want you doing anything dangerous. If you must play on a sled, then please do so inside the castle garden." He marched away down the corridor.

"But there are no hills to slide down inside the castle garden," said Freya softly.

But King Eric had already gone.

Freya sat down on her bed, hugging Minky tightly. The kitten had now fallen fast asleep, and her tiny pink nose twitched, as if she was dreaming of pouncing on another brown foot mouse.

Clarabel sat down next to Freya and put an arm around her shoulders. "I'm sure they'll be all right in the shed. Your dad said they would be given plenty of food and water."

"But it won't be the same!" Freya's eyes filled with tears. "I won't be able to wake up in the morning and hug them right away, or let Minky play on my bed."

"Let's cuddle them now, before they have to go," said Lulu, picking up one of the furry black kittens.

Emily and Jaminta picked up a kitten each, and then Clarabel hugged the last two.

"They're so warm and soft." Freya nuzzled Minky's black ears. "I hate to think of them out there in the castle shed surrounded by ice and snow."

CHAPTER FOUR

The Secret Feast

That evening, there was a royal banquet
in the Great Hall. The fire roared and
golden flames reached up to the top
of the fireplace. The long table was
decorated with candles and sprigs of
holly. A delicious roast dinner was served,
but Freya was too worried to enjoy it.

She rushed away as soon as dinner
was over, not even bothering to have
any dessert. As she climbed the stairs,
her long, pale blue dress floated out

around her ankles. She wore her favorite tiara, which was shaped like glittering snowflakes made of silver. The snow-quartz pendant hung on its long blue ribbon around her neck.

Freya opened the door to her bedroom and found the place quiet and empty. The mother cat and all the kittens had been moved. Sitting down on the bed, she gazed at the bare corner where the box had been. She knew her dad was angry about the hole in his slipper, but taking the kittens just seemed so unfair. Tears filled her eyes, and she wiped them on the back of her hand.

There was a knock at the open door and Clarabel's head peeked around. "Can we come in? We've got something that might cheer you up."

Freya nodded, trying to smile.

Clarabel came in, followed by Lulu,

Emily, and Jaminta. The princesses' colored dresses swirled around them as they sat down on the bed. Their tiaras shone in the soft lamplight.

"We brought strawberry zingers." Lulu showed Freya a paper bag full of sugary red sweets.

"And fruit snacks and chocolate," added Jaminta.

"We thought a midnight feast might keep you from feeling sad," explained Emily.

Freya smiled gratefully. "You're all so nice. I'm all right. I know my dad thinks the kittens will be safe and happy in the castle shed. It's just . . ." She bit her lip.

"What's wrong?" asked Emily.

"I don't know if the shed will be warm enough. The gardener keeps a little heater in there, but it doesn't work very well. I don't think my dad realizes that." Freya's forehead creased with worry.

A light pattering began on the window pane. The girls twisted around to look at the pale snowflakes falling past the glass.

"Have some chocolate to cheer you up," said Lulu, handing Freya a whole bar.

"I think we should go down to the shed and check on the kittens," said Clarabel, curling her golden hair behind her ear. "That way we'll know they're all right in their new home."

Lulu's eyes gleamed. "If we wait until everyone's in bed, then no one will see us. . . ."

"And we can use ninja moves!" said Jaminta.

"Great! That's decided, then," said Lulu, and she popped a strawberry zinger into her mouth and crunched it.

"What *are* your ninja moves?" asked Freya, nibbling a corner of her chocolate bar.

Emily grinned. "It's easier to show you!" She took four fruit snacks and put them in Freya's hand. "Just wait here and keep your eyes open!"

So Freya sat and waited, with four gummies in the palm of her hand, while the other princesses disappeared from the room. The falling snow grew heavier against the window. Then Freya suddenly felt something brush her hand lightly — Emily was standing there in her pink dress, holding one of the treats!

"How did you do that?" cried Freya. "I didn't see or hear you come back in."

"Well, that's the whole point." Emily grinned. "Ninja moves let you go anywhere without people noticing. Let's see how the others do."

Next, Jaminta appeared in her green silk dress, followed by Clarabel, wearing dark blue. Neither of them made a sound,

and two more candies disappeared from Freya's hand.

Finally, Lulu came into the room, but she ruined her perfect ninja move with a sneeze.

"Oops!" she laughed, tugging her wavy black hair. "That wasn't supposed to happen!"

"You were all fantastic! I wish I could do that," said Freya.

"We'll teach you how to do it," Emily promised. "My maid, Ally, used to be an undercover agent who caught jewel thieves, so she taught us these ninja skills. We've been practicing ever since."

"One more thing," said Clarabel. "Now that you're a Rescue Princess, you'll need one of our magical rings." She took off her sapphire ring and gave it to Freya.

"Really? You want me to wear it?" Freya gazed at the dark blue jewel.

Clarabel smiled. "We don't have time to make another ring for you right now, so you can borrow mine."

"Thank you!" said Freya, sliding it onto her finger.

"Let's stay awake until all the grown-ups are asleep. Then we can meet in here before we go out to see the kittens," said Jaminta.

"Great idea —" began Emily. But she broke off as a scuffling noise came from behind the bedroom door.

The princesses all looked at one another. What was going on? Surely it couldn't be King Eric coming to speak to them again. Emily raced over to the door and pulled it open.

A small princess stood in the doorway, staring at them intently. She had tight red curls and inquisitive green eyes. Freya thought she looked a bit like Emily.

"What are you all doing in here? Do you have candy?" said the younger princess.

"Lottie! This has nothing to do with you! Mind your own business!" burst out Emily. "Here, have a strawberry zinger and *don't* tell Mom and Dad that we had candy in the bedroom."

Lottie popped the zinger in her mouth and looked at them thoughtfully. Then she went away down the hall.

"That's my little sister, Lottie." Emily sighed. "We'll have to be careful. If she sees us sneaking out later she'll want to come, too. She's too young *and* she'll make lots of noise."

"I can't believe we're really going out to see the kittens tonight," said Freya. "I wish it was bedtime already!"

CHAPTER FIVE

Snow Ninjas

The princesses tiptoed down the stairs just after the clock struck half past eleven.

Freya's eyes shone with excitement as she crept after the others. *The grown-ups must be fast asleep*, she thought. The castle lay in deep silence.

A faint orange light shone across the hallway, made by the glowing coals in the fireplace of the Great Hall. The princesses crept over to the coat stand.

They hurried into their coats, then sneaked out of the front door and closed it carefully behind them.

Snowflakes dropped softly onto their heads.

Jaminta took a beautiful emerald bracelet out of her pocket. It cast rays of light across the garden, turning the dancing snowflakes green.

"That's awesome," whispered Freya, admiring the magical bracelet.

"Thanks." Jaminta smiled.

"Jaminta makes most of the jewels that we use," explained Emily. "She comes from the kingdom of Onica, where they know how to shape each gem to make it magical."

"Let's take this with us." Lulu picked up a large snow shovel that was leaning up against the castle wall. "If the snow gets deep then it might come in handy."

Freya led them across the garden.

They walked silently, their boots sinking into the snow. After several minutes, they came to a wooden shed with small windows. Lulu cleared the snow away from the bottom of the door with the shovel. Then Freya unbolted it and held it open for the other princesses. Behind her, she could see the falling snow already filling up their footprints.

She stepped into the shed and switched on the light. Seven pairs of cats' eyes blinked at her from a box in one corner.

"There you are!" Freya rushed over and stroked each kitten in turn.

The box, with its lining of soft sweaters, was sandwiched between a wheelbarrow and a towering mass of plant pots. Some of the kittens began meowing when they saw Freya. Minky stood up, scrabbling at the air with her white paws.

"The king was right," said Jaminta. "There's plenty of water and cat food here."

"It does feel cold, though." Emily shivered.

Freya put her hand above the little heater to check for warmth. "The heater's running."

"Look!" Clarabel pointed at a pile of snow on the other side of the shed. "There's snow coming in over here."

There was a plate-sized hole in the roof that gave them a glimpse of the night sky. Snowflakes were slowly drifting through it, adding to the rising mound on the floor. As they looked up at the hole, a gust of wind blew the swirling flakes sideways into their faces.

"We can't leave the kittens here with that hole in the roof," said Lulu. "If the snow keeps falling like this, it will be really cold and wet by morning."

They all looked at Freya, who was twisting one blond braid anxiously around her finger.

"We can't take them back to my bedroom — my dad would be so mad," said Freya. "But maybe we could hide them in the laundry room. The only person who goes in there is our maid, Greta, and she won't tell if I ask her not to."

"Great idea! King Eric will never find them in there!" said Lulu.

"But how do we get them back inside?" asked Jaminta doubtfully. "If someone sees us, they'll know right away what we're doing."

"How about we hide the kittens under our coats?" suggested Clarabel. "That way we'll keep them warm and well hidden."

"We'll have to go there and back twice, I think," said Freya. "There are six kittens and their mom that have to be moved and it'll be too difficult carrying more than one at a time."

So Freya, Emily, Clarabel, and Lulu picked up one soft black kitten each. The little cats blinked at the girls and meowed pitifully about being taken away from their mother's warm fur. But they were soon snuggled up in the princesses' coats with only their eyes, ears, and little pink noses showing. Jaminta held the shed door open for them and shone her emerald bracelet across the snow to light the way.

They hurried into the castle and down the stone passageway that led to the laundry room. Inside, they found an empty laundry basket. They padded it with a soft towel and popped the four kittens into it. Then they returned to the shed to fetch the next batch of kittens.

This time Emily took the mother cat, Clarabel took another black kitten, and Lulu picked up the box they had been living in.

Freya looked around for Minky. She half laughed and half sighed when she found her. The little black-and-white kitten was climbing up the towering heap of plant pots. Her tiny front claws gripped the sides of the pots as her back legs began to slip.

"Minky! We don't have time for that!" said Freya, picking her up and slipping her into the top of her coat.

"Meow?" said Minky, fixing her blue eyes on Freya just like she was asking a question.

"We're taking you somewhere better," replied Freya. "You're so little. You need to stay somewhere warm."

"Meow!" Minky agreed.

The princesses took one last look at the thick snowflakes coming in through the hole in the roof. Then they closed the door and left the shed behind. The snow was falling faster now. The girls bowed their heads, trying to protect the kittens from the cold as much as they could. The trek across the garden seemed longer this time and Lulu had to grab Clarabel's arm to keep her from falling into a snowdrift.

When they reached the castle, they shook the snow from their hair. Jaminta tucked her glowing emerald bracelet in her pocket and they stepped inside.

The hallway was almost dark now. The glow from the fire had died away.

"At least we didn't have to hide from Lottie," whispered Emily. "I was sure she would try to stay awake to see what we were doing. She's such a nosy little sister sometimes!"

Just then, the stairs creaked and the princesses froze.

Freya peered up into the darkness, aware of little Minky hidden beneath her coat. What would she say if her dad came down to the hallway and saw them? They had come so close to saving the kittens from the cold. Surely nothing could spoil it now?

The creaking grew louder, as if there were lots of pairs of feet on the stairs. The princesses were caught by a beam from a flashlight. Voices whispered in the shadows.

"Who's that?" hissed Lulu, hiding the cat bed behind her back.

Footsteps came toward them, and three princes appeared. The prince at the front was tall, with a ruffled mop of blond hair. Freya remembered him from when she and her dad had greeted their guests the day before.

The blond-haired prince pointed his flashlight at them.

"Stop it, Olaf! I can't see!" snapped Lulu.

"Oops! Sorry Lulu!" said the prince, lowering his flashlight.

"I met you yesterday, didn't I?" said Freya.

The blond prince nodded. "That's right! And this is George and Dinesh." He pointed to the other princes, who stood behind him in their slippers and pajamas.

"What are you doing down here?" asked George. "We thought you were one of the grown-ups."

"Have you been outside?" asked Dinesh, looking at their soggy coats.

The snow on their clothes was melting and water dripped down onto the floor.

"We just went out to look at the snow," Freya said quickly. As she spoke, Minky began to wiggle under her coat.

Olaf frowned. He looked like he wanted to ask more questions, but Lulu butted in. "What are *you* doing here? And why are you sneaking around with a flashlight?" she asked fiercely.

The princes grinned at one another.

"We're going to the kitchen to find some chocolate cookies for a midnight feast," said Olaf. "Do you want to come with us?"

Freya could see a pink nose and a little set of whiskers quivering over the top of Clarabel's coat. She gave her a nudge.

"What's the matter?" asked Clarabel. Then she caught sight of her kitten and tried to hide it with her scarf.

Minky, who was tired of sitting still, let out a loud meow.

The princes stared at Freya in astonishment. Olaf lifted his light and pointed it toward her.

"Uhh!" Freya pretended to yawn to disguise another loud meow. She could feel Minky wiggling again. Any moment now, she half expected the kitten to jump out of her coat and gallop around the hallway.

Hearing her kitten, the mother cat stuck her nose out of Emily's coat and started meowing, too.

"Eeeh!" squealed Emily, quickly changing it to a pretend yawn to match Freya's.

The princes exchanged puzzled looks.

"Are you feeling all right?" Olaf asked Emily.

"Oh, yes! I'm just a little tired," explained Emily.

Then all the princesses joined in, putting their hands over their mouths and yawning loudly.

"Sorry! We're too tired for a midnight

feast," said Jaminta cheerfully. "Good night!"

Then the girls rushed away down the stone passageway, keeping their hands over their mouths to stop their laughter.

CHAPTER SIX

Skating Princesses

"I couldn't believe it when the kittens all started meowing!" said Clarabel as they reached the laundry room.

"I've never tried to yawn so loudly before!" giggled Emily. "I was sure they would figure out that we were hiding something!"

Lulu found a quiet corner to put the cat bed in. Then, one by one, they settled the mother cat and the kittens inside it. The kittens snuggled up to the warmth

of their mom. Even Minky seemed happy
to curl up and close her eyes after all the
excitement of rushing through the snow
while half hidden under Freya's coat.

The princesses tiptoed back to their
rooms as fast as they dared and
whispered good night to one another.
Freya lay down in her bed feeling much
happier than before. The kittens would
be warm and comfortable in the laundry
room. She would explain it all to her
maid, Greta, in the morning.

The next day, she jumped out of bed
as soon as she woke up. Opening her
wardrobe, she rummaged around for a
thick sweater and pants. They were all
going to skate on the ice rink today, so
she needed warm clothes.

She thought about the kittens as she got
dressed. What if her dad found them in

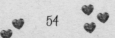

the laundry room? He didn't usually go in there. But what if he heard a noise and went to look? She had to try to talk to him about it. Not this morning — he would be too busy with his royal guests. But soon. Maybe she should hide the kittens a little better and wait for a good time to tell him.

She raced downstairs and into the laundry room. The mother cat was wide-awake and grooming her babies with her long pink tongue. Minky didn't seem to like being cleaned and jumped out of the box and scampered across the floor.

"No, Minky!" said Freya gently. "You can't run away." She picked up Minky and put her back in the box. Then she padded the sides with an extra towel to make it harder for the kittens to climb out.

A row of washing machines stood along one wall, with piles of folded sheets stacked on top. Freya picked one sheet off the top and hung it over the clothesline that stretched from one wall to the other. Quickly, she found two clothespins and pinned the sheet in place. She stood back and smiled. Now the sheet made a sort of screen to hide the kittens. No one who glanced in would notice them at all. Carefully, she closed the door to keep the kittens safe inside.

"Don't forget to take your gloves with you when you go ice skating, Freya," said King Eric, when Freya reached the Great Hall.

"Yes, Dad, I'll remember," replied Freya, hurriedly brushing black and white cat hairs off her sweater.

After a breakfast of scrambled eggs and muffins, the kings, queens, princes, and princesses put on their coats and headed outdoors. Freya found Emily excitedly pulling on her snow boots.

"I've never been ice skating before," Emily said excitedly. "Is it hard?"

"You have to get used to the ice," said Freya. "After that, it's really easy."

They held hands and ran across the castle garden and down the snowy hill together. They stopped at the bottom, laughing as they tried to catch their breath. The ice rink lay ahead of them, shining like a mirror in the sunshine.

King Eric clapped his hands. "Listen, please, everyone," he called. "This ice rink is perfectly safe, but you must *not* skate over there on the river." He pointed to a glittering river beyond the farthest end of the rink. "The river ice is thin in some places and that makes it *very* dangerous. Does everyone understand?"

Everyone looked at the river in the distance and nodded.

Jaminta, Lulu, and Clarabel came running over to Freya and Emily.

"I can't wait to put my skates on!" cried Lulu. "This is *so* exciting!"

"Look at me!" yelled Prince Olaf, who was already out on the ice. He tried to spin around and around, but lost his balance and crash-landed on his bottom.

The princesses giggled.

"Don't worry, I'm fine," he said, picking himself up and grinning.

Freya found them all ice skates to wear. Then she helped a nervous Clarabel onto the ice.

"Show us how to ice skate, Freya," called Jaminta.

Freya smiled. She loved skating. She glided into a clear space and performed a perfect figure eight. Then she showed

them her backward skating and finished off with a long pirouette.

"That was awesome!" said Lulu.

"Thanks!" Freya smiled.

The ice rink filled up with skaters. The younger princes and princesses held on to their mom or dad to help them balance. All except Emily's sister, Lottie, who skated into the middle of the ice and spun around fearlessly.

"Look, Emily!" said Freya. "Your sister's really good at this."

"Really?" said Emily in surprise. "I hope she doesn't start showing off."

Lottie smiled as she glided past them and performed another spin.

After a while, large snowflakes began drifting slowly down. The grown-ups called everyone off the ice rink. The princesses took off their skates and climbed the hill back to the castle.

"I bet my dad will have mugs of hot chocolate ready for everyone," said Freya, smiling.

"I love hot chocolate!" said Emily.

The princesses rubbed their cold hands together and climbed a little faster. They reached the castle door ahead of everyone else.

But as the door swung open, there was no delicious hot chocolate smell and no roaring fire in the Great Hall. There was only a rumbling noise coming from the direction of the kitchens.

It was her dad's voice, Freya realized, and he didn't sound very happy.

King Eric burst through the kitchen door into the hallway.

"Where did it go?" He looked around wildly. "I'll catch it right now! I won't have that furry little pest running around everywhere."

"What happened?" whispered Clarabel.

Freya stared at her dad's angry face. Suddenly, she knew exactly what was going on, and her heart sank.

One of the kittens must have escaped from the laundry room, and that meant she and the kitten were both in very deep trouble.

The Wandering Kitten

"There's a kitten cavorting around this castle!" said the king sternly. "Did you move the animals from the shed? Tell me the truth, Freya!"

But before Freya could answer, Greta hurried along the passageway. She was wearing a white apron and carrying a laundry basket. "It's all my fault, Your Majesty," she said breathlessly. "I tried to keep the laundry-room door shut so they couldn't escape, but one spirited little thing sneaked past me when I came in with some washing."

"It is *not* your fault, Greta," said King Eric. "The kittens should not have been inside the castle at all. I had forbidden it! Freya, it *must* have been you who moved them!"

"Yes, I did move them," said Freya. "But only because they were so cold in the shed last night. There was a hole in the roof and —"

"Last night!" barked the king. "You went wandering outside in the middle of the night! You are NOT allowed to do that, Freya!"

"We only went out into the garden," said Lulu. "And we took a snow shovel with us."

The hallway fell silent. King Eric's face turned deep red.

Freya was desperately wondering how to explain the whole thing and make her dad understand why she'd moved the kittens. If only he would listen! Then she heard little paws scampering along the wooden floor of the Great Hall.

"That's the kitten!" exclaimed the king. "Now I'll catch the silly creature! Then they'll all go back in the shed where they belong!" He darted through the doorway.

By now, many of the kings, queens, and younger princes and princesses had reached the castle. They poured into the hallway behind Freya. A murmur of astonishment rose from the crowd as they looked at King Eric.

The king was running up and down the Great Hall, his arms outstretched. Ahead of him skipped a tiny black-and-white kitten.

Minky paused now and then to meow at the king as if urging him to run faster. Then she scrambled under the chairs and appeared on the other side of the long table. Her tail was pointed into the air and her ears were pricked up. She looked as if she was enjoying the chasing game enormously.

The crowd of kings and queens smiled in amusement at the little kitten.

"Minky! Come here!" called Freya. If she got to Minky first, then maybe she could talk to her dad and explain everything.

But Minky swished her tail and scampered away.

Just then, King Eric sneaked around the table and made a grab for the kitten.

Frightened, Minky jumped onto the table and dashed along it, sending plates and napkins flying. Then she leapt off the end and ran straight between the king's legs and across the hallway.

"No!" yelled the king.

Freya ran through the crowd and stopped at the open door. Where was Minky?

Now that the show was over, the crowd of kings and queens began to move into the Great Hall, talking about coffee and lunch.

A gray-haired queen tapped Freya on the elbow. "The little animal escaped, my dear. Out there." She pointed at the snowy garden.

Freya stared across the snow in dismay. How had Minky disappeared so fast? Was that a black-and-white kitten scampering down the hill?

She stepped out into the freezing garden, not caring that she didn't have her coat on. She still couldn't see any sign of Minky. An icy fear grew inside her. Minky was in danger, out here all alone. It wasn't a good place for a kitten to be.

"Freya!" Emily hurried over to her. "Are you OK?"

Freya looked at the kings and queens walking away. It felt like they were deliberately turning their backs on Minky. "Where are they all going?" she cried. "Don't they know that a kitten can't survive for long out in the snow?"

King Eric reached the doorway. "Freya! I would like to talk to you!"

Freya turned pink. "I can't! I have to find Minky right now! What if she gets lost or stuck in a snowdrift?" She darted back inside, grabbed her coat from the house, and then ran out across the garden and through the castle gate. Freya raced down the hill, only stopping at the bottom

to search the snowy ground for signs of the kitten.

The snow had stopped falling, but the air felt colder than before. Freya's breath hung in front of her in a little misty cloud.

She scanned the hillside again and looked closely at the ice rink. She couldn't see Minky anywhere.

"Hold on, Freya!" said Lulu, as the other princesses ran to catch up with her.

"We'll look for Minky, too," said Emily.

Clarabel put her arm around Freya. "You're a Rescue Princess now! That means you've got friends to help you."

Freya's eyes filled with tears. "Oh, thank you! I'm just so worried about her. She's so small and she doesn't know about all the dangers out here. What if she meets a wild animal?"

"Look! This will help us." Jaminta pointed at a patch of ground.

The others ran over to look. Tiny marks zigzagged across the snow in front of them.

"Paw prints!" exclaimed Emily. "Good job, Jaminta! That means Minky must have come this way."

"Are you sure those tracks were really made by a kitten and not a snow rabbit or something?" said Lulu.

Freya crouched down next to the tracks and traced a finger around one print with its circle and four little pads. "These paw prints were definitely made by a kitten," she said. "Quick! Let's follow them!"

CHAPTER EIGHT

The Tracks in the Snow

The princesses ran at full speed,
following the tracks in the snow. The
paw prints led them right down to
the place where they'd ice skated that
morning. They looked around anxiously.
On one side was the glittering ice rink
and on the other was a forest of fir trees.
But there was still no sign of Minky.

"Look at these tracks. She must have
run around in circles!" said Emily,
pointing to the scrambled-up paw prints.

The girls ran this way and that, trying to follow the direction of the tracks. But they crisscrossed in so many places that it was hard to figure out which way the little cat had gone.

"Stop, everyone!" called Freya. "If we keep running, we'll end up trampling over all the marks in the snow. Then we'll never find Minky."

The princesses stood still, looking anxiously at one another.

Freya caught a flash of movement near the fir trees and stepped toward it. But it was only a squirrel, darting across the snow and running up the trunk of the nearest tree.

"Let's split up and look for Minky in different places," suggested Jaminta. "Some of the tracks go down to the ice rink. Lulu and I could look there, while you three search those trees." She pointed at the forest of fir trees.

"All right, then! Let's meet back here in a few minutes," said Emily.

Freya, Emily, and Clarabel hurried into the trees, following the paw prints closely. Nothing moved in the forest, and the crunching of their boots sounded loud in the silent woods.

"We should look up into the trees as well as on the ground," said Freya. "Maybe Minky's climbed onto a branch and gotten stuck."

The girls peered up at the fir trees, which were covered with a thick blanket of snow.

"Can you hear anything?" asked Emily.

They all listened for a moment, but heard nothing except the birds singing.

They followed the paw prints, which circled around and led them over to the edge of the forest again.

"Now we're back where we started!"

Freya cried. "Why can't we find her?" Tears filled her eyes and she rushed out of the forest.

As she ran out of the trees, Jaminta and Lulu ran toward her from the opposite direction.

"We couldn't find her down by the ice rink," said Lulu. "Did you have any luck?"

Freya shook her head and sniffed.

Clarabel and Emily ran out of the trees behind them.

"I don't think Minky is in there," panted Emily. "I'm sure we would have heard her meowing."

"What should we do?" asked Clarabel.

"Let's look at the paw prints again," said Jaminta.

"No! That didn't work before," said Emily urgently. "The paw prints are too messed up and they just go around in circles."

"I think we should try following them one more time," said Jaminta. "What do you think, Freya?"

Freya tugged at her braid anxiously. But before she could decide, a large snowflake drifted down and landed on her coat. Then there was another and another, until the air was full of dancing flakes.

Freya pulled up her hood. "This snow will cover up the paw prints, anyway. So I think we should keep looking for her and calling out, and hope she calls back."

"Let's go toward the river," said Emily, pointing straight ahead. "We haven't looked over there yet."

They hurried along the side of the ice rink, scanning its shiny surface and calling Minky's name. Freya trudged on, her heart sinking with every second. Minky would be cold and scared by now, and the falling snow made it so much harder to see.

They reached the end of the ice rink, where the river curved past and wound away into the distance like a great glittering snake.

"Minky?" bellowed Lulu. "Can you hear us?" Her call bounced off the hills and echoed back at her.

"Did you hear that?" asked Freya, suddenly.

"It's a good echo, isn't it?" agreed Lulu, wiping snow off her black hair.

"No! Not the echo," said Freya. "Listen!"

The princesses listened carefully. At last they heard a tiny meow drifting across the ice and snow.

"That *must* be Minky!" breathed Clarabel. "We've found her at last!"

CHAPTER NINE

The Frozen River

The princesses grinned at one another.

"We're coming, Minky!" called Freya. "Don't worry!"

Another meow drifted over to them, a little louder this time.

"I think she knows it's you calling, Freya," said Clarabel.

"But where is she? Where's the sound coming from?" wondered Lulu.

They all listened again.

"It's over here!" Freya rushed excitedly down the slope to the riverbank. Her blond braids bobbed up and down as she ran. She passed a small rowboat that lay on the bank, covered with snow, and stopped right at the edge of the river.

The other princesses followed her, holding their hoods up against the falling snow.

"Minky? Where are you?" Freya peered through the swirling whiteness.

"Is there something in that tree?" asked Emily.

"Yes! I can see something, too!" cried Clarabel.

Freya's heart lifted as they sprinted over to the birch tree. It grew right on the edge of the riverbank and the snow lined its thin branches. As they got closer, a branch halfway up the tree began to wobble, and a whiskery face peered down.

"Meow!" Minky gazed sadly at them from a narrow branch that stretched out over the icy river. She crouched down low and the branch swayed with every swish of her tail.

"Oh, Minky!" said Freya. "Why did you go up there? Were you trying to chase a bird or something?"

The snow stopped falling and the clouds disappeared, making way for bright sunshine. The princesses pulled back their hoods and looked up at the little kitten.

"Jump down, Minky! You can do it," called Lulu.

Minky's tail swished harder.

"She's too scared to jump," said Clarabel. "Don't worry, Minky. We'll get you down."

Freya stood on tiptoe, stretching up as high as she could, but Minky's branch

was on the other side of the tree trunk, a long way out of reach.

"She's too far away," said Freya. "Come closer, Minky."

But Minky just stared at them, unblinking. Her little paws gripped tightly onto the thin branch.

"I know!" said Lulu. "I'll just climb up onto these lower branches and grab her." She put her foot on the lowest branch. But as soon as she tried to pull herself up, the whole tree shook alarmingly and Minky let out a frightened yowl.

"Sorry!" Lulu backed away hastily.

Freya bit her lip. This wasn't going to be easy.

Emily picked her way down the sloping bank to the edge of the ice. "If I walk out onto the river, I should be able to reach up to her branch."

"But Freya's dad told us that the river ice is really thin," Lulu reminded her.

"I'll only stand on it for a few seconds," said Emily. She went to put a foot on the ice when Freya's voice made her jump.

"Stop, Emily!" called Freya. "It's much too dangerous!" She pulled her friend back. "I'll show you how thin it really is. Watch this!"

Freya picked up a pebble and threw it onto the river. As it landed, lines split across the surface as the ice began to break.

"You're right!" gasped Emily. "I didn't realize how easily it would crack."

"We'll have to find another way to reach Minky," said Jaminta.

"But what *can* we do?" said Clarabel. "We don't have time to get a ladder."

Minky swished her tail, sending snow sprinkling down.

Freya stared at Minky's branch, which was now bare of snow. "Oh, no!" she gasped. "Look at where the branch meets the tree trunk!"

"What's wrong?" asked Lulu.

"There's a split there." Freya pointed up to the branch.

As the princesses watched, the crack widened and the branch sagged as if it was tired of holding up Minky's weight.

"Minky's too heavy," cried Clarabel. "If that split gets any bigger, the branch will fall. . . ."

"And Minky will land on the ice just like that pebble," finished Lulu.

Freya put her hand to her mouth. She had to get Minky down before the branch broke. But how?

CHAPTER TEN

Freya's Letter

Minky meowed at them unhappily and tried to edge along the branch.

"Stay still, Minky!" said Freya urgently.

But Minky didn't understand. She scratched at the branch with her claws. Every movement made the tree sway and the split grow a little wider. Below, the river ice waited.

"Stay really still, Minky, or you'll make it worse," called Freya. "Oh, I wish we could do something about this awful ice."

She leaned forward and the blue ribbon around her neck fell free of her coat and dangled down.

Jaminta stared at the beautiful snow-quartz jewel that hung on the end of the ribbon. "What was it you said before about your jewel, Freya?"

Freya glanced down. "Oh, you mean the snow quartz that my mom left for me?"

"Yes, you said there was a note from your mom about it," said Jaminta.

"There's no time for all that jewel stuff," interrupted Lulu. "We need a way to get the kitten down!"

"But it might be important," said Jaminta, with a frown. "We've used jewels to help us with rescues before."

"Please don't start arguing," pleaded Clarabel. "Let's just think about Minky."

Freya put one hand on the tree trunk. "I think I should try to climb up," she

said, with a tremble in her voice. "I'm smaller than you, Lulu, so maybe I won't shake the tree so much."

Lulu nodded. "You are a bit smaller than me, and Minky won't be so frightened if it's you."

"Be careful!" said Clarabel. "The whole tree will be slippery because of all the snow."

Freya smiled weakly and lifted her foot up onto the lowest branch. The tree wobbled a little, but she found the next foothold and continued. Minky peered down, her whiskers quivering.

Freya reached for the next branch and the next. Her arms began to ache. This was even harder than she'd expected it to be.

She paused for a second, resting her cheek against the rough tree trunk.

Snap! The sound made her gasp. She
tilted backward to look at Minky's
branch. It was still there! She sighed
with relief and looked down at the other
princesses.

"You're doing great! Keep going!" called
Clarabel.

But Freya didn't hear Clarabel's words.
Her heart was thumping as she looked
at the ground. It was so far away! How
would she ever get down again?

She shut her eyes for a second and took
a deep breath. She shouldn't look down
anymore. It was just making her nervous.

She opened her eyes and stretched out
for the next branch, but as she tried to
pull herself up she felt something tugging
on her neck. The blue ribbon that held
her snow jewel was caught on a twig.
As she moved, the ribbon broke and the
snow quartz fell.

"Oh, no! My necklace fell off!" she called down to the others, remembering not to look at the ground.

"Don't worry, we'll find it!" called Emily.

Freya wasn't sure how they were going to spot a white jewel in the middle of all that snow. But she had to concentrate on reaching Minky. She was just about to continue climbing when Lulu shouted.

At the same moment, the branch Freya was standing on snapped. She slipped and tumbled down, just managing to catch ahold of a lower branch to save herself. The tree shook and Minky meowed pitifully.

"Freya! Are you OK?" Clarabel helped her climb off the bottom branch and onto the ground again.

Freya stood in the snow, her legs trembling. "I guess that branch wasn't very strong!" she said shakily. "Thanks for helping me, Clarabel."

She looked over at the others. Why were they staring at a patch of snow?

"Freya, come and look at this!" Lulu motioned her over. "See what your jewel is doing."

Freya moved closer. There was a gap in the snow and her jewel lay right in the middle. As she watched, the snow around the quartz melted, making the hole wider and deeper. Grass showed through at the bottom.

"What's happening?" Freya picked up the snow quartz. It felt warm in her hand.

"Freya, do you have the letter your mother left you?" asked Jaminta urgently.

Freya held up the snow jewel, which caught the sunlight and gleamed. "Yes. I always keep it in my pocket."

"Can I see it?" asked Jaminta.

Freya nodded and fumbled in her pants pocket. She brought out a piece of paper, crinkled with age, and unfolded it.

Dear Freya,
This snow quartz is my favorite jewel and I'm giving it to you. It will protect you from ice and snow. I hope one day you'll find it useful. Wear it always and think of me.
With all my love,
Mom xxx

" 'It will protect you from ice and snow,' " murmured Clarabel. "What does that mean?"

"I've never really been sure," said Freya.

"It melted *this* snow," said Emily excitedly. "So maybe it can melt *all* ice and snow!"

Jaminta nodded. "I think this jewel is extremely magical."

"But how will that help us save Minky?" wondered Clarabel.

Freya frowned, then her face brightened. "What about that boat? If the jewel melts the ice then we can take it out on the river. That way we can get closer to Minky!" She pointed at the little rowboat that lay a few yards away on the riverbank.

"Great idea!" said Lulu. "Try touching the river ice with the snow jewel. Let's see if it works."

The branch creaked, and Minky gave a long and mournful yowl.

"We'd better hurry!" said Clarabel. "I don't think Minky's branch will hold much longer."

Freya crouched down on the edge of the bank and held the snow jewel above the river. Gently, she lowered the rough-shaped quartz until it brushed against the ice. The jewel filled with a fierce brightness, whiter than any snow.

The princesses held their breath.

Little by little, the ice turned to water. A small blue puddle formed all around the place where the snow jewel touched the river. It grew bigger and bigger as the ice melted into nothing.

"That's amazing!" said Emily.

"I didn't know my jewel could do that," whispered Freya. "It really *is* magic."

CHAPTER ELEVEN

The Kitten and the Jewel

Freya held the sparkling jewel steady against the frozen river. The ice retreated even farther, turning the river a watery blue.

"Let's get the boat ready!" said Emily.

Emily, Clarabel, Lulu, and Jaminta ran over to the rowboat and lifted it up. They carried it back across the snow, staggering under its bulky weight.

The wind blew against the bare branches of Minky's tree, and the kitten meowed louder and louder.

Freya jumped up and tucked the snow quartz into her pocket. How much longer would that tree branch hold?

"Let's get this boat into the water!" Lulu shouted. "Ready, set, go!"

The boat landed in the river with a splash, and Lulu launched herself in after it. Clarabel held on to the side of the boat to let Freya, Emily, and Jaminta climb in. Then she pushed the boat away from the bank as hard as she could.

"Thanks, Clarabel!" called Freya.

Lulu and Jaminta grabbed an oar each from the bottom of the boat and paddled hard. They rowed toward the place where Minky's branch hung over the freezing cold water.

The kitten peered down at them. Her branch wobbled and she scrabbled to hold on with her tiny claws.

"We need to get closer!" said Emily.

Lulu and Jaminta rowed faster and faster.

"Hold on, Minky," said Freya. "We're almost there."

But Minky had no more strength left in her paws. She slipped and fell. Freya held out her hands and Minky landed softly in her arms just as the rowboat glided underneath the tree.

Freya hugged her tight. "Minky! I've got you at last! You feel so cold!"

The kitten's black-and-white fur was freezing cold from crouching on the snowy branch, and ice crystals hung on the end of her whiskers.

Jaminta and Lulu rowed back toward the riverbank. The ice had melted all the way across, and a whole stretch of river water sparkled in the winter sun.

The boat reached the shore, and Freya handed Minky to Clarabel, who took off

her coat and wrapped the tiny kitten
up in it.

"Is she all right?" asked Emily.

Freya bit her lip. "She could get very sick
if we don't warm her up fast enough."
She stroked Minky's fur, feeling the icy
patches on her head and tummy. She
rubbed them gently with Clarabel's coat,
but more ice kept forming. The kitten
suddenly seemed very small and thin.

"Try the snow jewel again!" said
Jaminta eagerly. "It's supposed to protect
against ice and snow. Maybe it will work
on Minky."

So Clarabel held Minky still while
Freya touched her fur with the snow
quartz. The patches of ice melted away,
leaving the kitten's fur soft and dry
beneath.

"Oh, that's better!" said Freya. "Feel her
fur now; she's as warm as a blanket!"

The princesses crowded around Minky, scratching her ears and her fluffy belly.

"You're right, she feels beautifully warm and soft now!" cried Lulu.

"Minky, you scared us all!" said Emily, stroking the kitten's little pink nose.

Minky pricked up her ears and her blue eyes shone.

"Let's take her back to the castle and sit by the fire," said Clarabel. "Then we can make sure that she's completely warmed up."

The princesses began the long walk past the ice rink and up the hill. They were very tired now and were glad when they reached the castle door. Checking that no one was watching, they hurried upstairs with Minky.

Lulu went in search of Greta, who agreed to light a fire in Freya's bedroom fireplace.

"I bet you've been running around in the cold and doing all kinds of foolish things," Greta scolded as she got the flames going.

"Minky got stuck in a tree," said Freya meekly. "We had to help her."

"Well, you've probably caught a cold now," said Greta, shaking her head. "You'd better have something hot to drink." Greta hurried away to the kitchen to retrieve some hot chocolate.

Minky yawned widely, showing her tiny white teeth and pink tongue. Then she curled up in Freya's arms and went to sleep. Her white tummy rose and fell peacefully.

"What a happy end to the day." Lulu yawned. "I wish it was nighttime. I don't think I can stay awake through another banquet."

"I don't think I can, either!" Jaminta turned to Freya. "What a surprise that your snow quartz turned out to be such a magical jewel!"

Freya smiled and threaded the white stone back onto its blue ribbon. "It's even more special to me now. My mom must have known I would need its help one day, and she was right!"

Just then, Greta came back with five mugs of hot chocolate, five plates, and a large round cherry cake.

"What a lovely cake!" said Emily. "You're very nice to us, Greta!"

"Humph! Just don't tell the cook I gave it to you," said Greta. "And no more chasing after animals in the snow! Although you *are* sweet girls to worry so much about a little creature." Greta tickled Minky under the chin.

Freya twisted a blond braid around one finger. "Greta? Have you seen my dad since this morning?"

"Yes, I saw him just now," replied Greta. "He sent for you, as a matter of fact. You're to go and see him in the library right now."

"Do you think he'll be mad at you, Freya?" asked Clarabel, wide-eyed.

Freya made a face. "Probably! But I have to try and make him understand. The kittens are so important to me. I had to make sure they were safe." She kissed Minky's soft black-and-white fur.

CHAPTER TWELVE

The Royal Academy for Princesses

Freya walked down the corridor with
Minky still fast asleep in her arms.
Now and then the kitten let out a tiny
murmuring meow, as if she was having
happy dreams of chasing mice.

Freya stopped outside a door with a
large golden doorknob and bit her lip.
All she could do was explain what had
happened and hope her dad would
understand. She knocked softly on the
door and went in.

Her dad was sitting in a green leather armchair, reading a book. His golden crown was perched lopsidedly on top of his head. Behind him, shelves full of books stretched across the wall.

King Eric closed his book with a *snap* and frowned at her. "Freya, what on earth is going on? I thought I told you that the kittens should stay in the garden shed from now on."

Freya took a step toward him. "But when we went to see them, we saw a big hole in the roof and the snow was coming in. We couldn't leave the kittens there. It was freezing!"

King Eric's frown deepened. "So you brought them back inside. Is that why one of them was running around the Great Hall this morning? It was very embarrassing having to chase her in front of our guests."

Minky woke up and pricked up her ears. With a little shake of her head, she jumped down from Freya's arms and padded over to King Eric. The king drew in his robes and tutted sharply. Minky leapt up onto his lap, turned around three times, and then settled down and purred.

King Eric stared at the bundle of black-and-white fur on his lap in complete surprise. Freya pressed her lips together, trying not to laugh.

Almost without meaning to, King Eric brought his hand up and scratched Minky gently between the ears.

"Well, Freya," he said gruffly. "I have decided that the garden shed is a totally unsuitable place for such young animals. The mother cat and her kittens must stay in the laundry room from now on."

"Thanks, Dad!" Freya beamed.

"And as for spending your time running around with these other princesses," King Eric continued, "I've made a decision about that, too."

"Oh, Dad!" cried Freya. "I love being with the other princesses. They're so much fun! I wish I could see them all the time."

"Well, I have some good news for you, then," said her dad. "I've been talking to the other kings and queens and they've told me about a Royal Academy for Princesses that's just right for girls your age. How would you like to go?"

"A princess school!" Freya gasped. "I'd love to!"

The king smiled at her, his eyes twinkling.

Minky stirred and let out a long meow, as if she was asking a question.

Freya's happy face clouded over. "Oh, dear! I'll miss you so much, Minky!"

"Actually, she can go, too," said King Eric. "The academy lets each princess bring a pet, as long as it isn't something too difficult to take care of."

"Really?" squealed Freya. "That's fantastic!"

"Now you must go and get ready for the banquet," said the king. "Take this kitten with you." He gave Minky one final stroke before handing her back.

Freya rushed back down the hallway. She felt like she was running on air. Soon she would be going to the Royal Academy for Princesses, and Minky would be coming, too!

When she opened the door, she found her bedroom empty. The other girls had probably gone to get dressed for the banquet, she thought. Putting Minky on her bed, she hurried to the wardrobe and pulled out a long, pale blue dress that floated down to her ankles. She put it on and added her snowflake tiara. Then she looked in the mirror.

She noticed how her snow quartz glittered on the end of its long ribbon.

It was strange to think that the jewel had always been there looking out for her, just as her mom had meant it to.

"Thanks, Mom," Freya whispered, and for a moment the gem seemed to glow a little brighter.

There was a knock at the door and Emily, Clarabel, Lulu, and Jaminta came in. Their dresses rustled as they moved. Emily wore a pink dress with red velvet flowers, Clarabel's dress was dark blue, and Jaminta's was made from smooth green silk. Lulu came in last, wearing a yellow dress dotted with sequins.

"I wish we didn't have to go home tomorrow," said Clarabel, smiling at

Freya. "I like Northernland — especially the sledding!"

"I'd better give you this ring back." Freya slid the sapphire ring off her finger and handed it to Clarabel. "I'm going away to the Royal Academy for Princesses soon, so I don't think I'll be able to use it."

"That's funny!" Clarabel smiled at her. "I'm going to the academy, too. My mom's just told me that I'm starting right after the holidays."

"That's where I'm going, too!" Lulu grinned. "My mom says I'm exactly the right age to join."

"Me, too!" said Jaminta. "That's really strange! How about you, Emily?"

"Yes, I'm going, too," replied Emily. "I'm really excited!"

"Then we'll all be together!" said Clarabel, squeezing Freya's hand.

Jaminta sat down heavily on the bed. "But what will we do about being Rescue Princesses? Once we're busy at the Royal Academy, we won't be able to leave school to perform rescues all the time. Who will help animals in trouble?"

There was silence while all the princesses thought about this.

"I think," said Emily slowly, "before we go, we should teach some other girls how to be Rescue Princesses."

Clarabel nodded. "That way someone can still be around to help animals in danger."

"But not just any princesses. They have to be brave and kind," said Jaminta.

"And want to learn acrobatics," added Lulu.

"Do we know any other princesses like that?" asked Jaminta doubtfully.

There was a swift knock and Emily's sister, Lottie, poked her head around the door. She was wearing a crimson dress. A crown dotted with rubies perched on top of her tight red curls.

"King Eric says you have to hurry up. They want to start the banquet." Lottie stared at them, her green eyes wide. "What are you all doing, anyway?"

"Don't start asking millions of questions!" cried Emily. "It's a secret!"

"Fine, then! But I'm going to find out one day. Just you wait!" Lottie gave them a determined look before she closed the door.

Freya looked thoughtful. "Maybe you should try telling Lottie about all of this. She might like to have some adventures."

"You mean tell her our secret?" said Emily, surprised. "But she's just my annoying sister."

A floorboard creaked outside in the hallway.

"I think you should tell her, too," said Clarabel, and the others nodded.

"After all, every girl deserves the chance to be a Rescue Princess," said Freya.

The door burst open and Lottie fixed her bright green eyes on Freya. "What's a Rescue Princess?" she asked.

Can't wait for
the Rescue Princesses's next
daring animal adventure?

The Magic Rings

Turn the page for
a sneak peek!

CHAPTER ONE

Royal Sisters

Princess Lottie spun around the bedroom as fast as she could, her red dress swirling. She turned around and around, until she got so dizzy that she collapsed, laughing, on top of the velvet blanket.

"Stop it, Lottie!" exclaimed Princess Emily. "You're squishing all the things I was just about to pack."

Lottie yanked a pile of creased clothes out from underneath her. Then she bounced up to peer into the enormous suitcase that lay next to her on the bed. It was full of dresses, tiaras, and a hairbrush with a diamond-studded handle.

"You can't fit anything else in there anyway," she said bluntly. "How much stuff do you need at your Royal School Thingy?"

"The Royal Academy for Princesses," Emily corrected her. "You have to have clothes for lessons, clothes for parties, clothes for ceremonies, and much more. I'll need all of these. There'll be so many special occasions to go to."

Lottie yawned. "Poor you! It sounds boring. I hope I don't have to go when I'm older."

Emily frowned. "It's important for every princess to learn how to fulfil her duties you know."

Lottie chuckled. "You sound just like Mom." She tried out a fancy accent.

"*A princess must perform splendid and magnificent duties, like spinning around as many times as she can before she falls over!*" She leapt off the bed and started twirling again.

"Lottie! Stop it!" groaned Emily. Then she sat down on her bed and sighed.

Lottie stopped spinning and landed beside her sister, making the bed wobble.

"I guess I do sound a little bit like Mom," said Emily. "I still like having fun, though, and I'm going to be seeing all my friends at the academy."

"I'll miss you!" Lottie gave her sister a quick hug. "Even though you like to whine!"

"I'll miss you, too." Emily grinned. "Even though you squish my clothes!"

Lottie looked at the mirror on the wall, where their reflections sat side by side.

Everybody always said it was easy to

tell that they were sisters, mainly because their hair was exactly the same red color, like a flame. But while Emily's hair hung over her shoulders in loose waves, Lottie's was clustered into tight curls. Their eyes were different, too. Lottie's were a bright sparkling green while Emily's were a gentler hazel.

Lottie had always wished she was the older one. But now she was glad she wasn't leaving for school. Emily said the academy would be exciting, but Lottie wasn't so sure.

"If you've left any tiaras behind, can I borrow them while you're gone?" asked Lottie, itching to look in Emily's closet.

But Emily wasn't listening. She gazed thoughtfully at her sister, twisting a lock of red hair around her finger.

"Why are you staring at me like that?"

asked Lottie. "I promise I'll put the tiaras back. I know I broke that silver one. But that was a long time ago."

"There's something I need to tell you," said Emily slowly. "You know when you heard me and my friends talking about being Rescue Princesses when we were staying in Northernland?"

"Yes, it sounded like a really good game." Lottie pouted. "And I think you should have let me join from the start."

"It wasn't a game at all," said Emily. "I was just worried that you were too little to know about it."

"I am NOT little!" Lottie burst out.

"I guess not." Emily smiled. "Now that you've had your birthday, you're the same age as I was when I first became a Rescue Princess! Jaminta, Clarabel, and Lulu have all sent me their magic rings, so I can explain that part, too."

"What?" Lottie nearly bounced off the bed. "What magic rings?"

"Hold on! I need to tell you everything from the beginning," said Emily. "Just listen! And try not to interrupt!"

Lottie frowned, but then decided not to be impatient. After all, she wanted to know what Emily was going to say. "Tell me, then. What's this Rescue Princesses thing all about?"